The Jam Panda
Red Story Book

The Jam Panda

Red Story Book

Written by Caroline Repchuk
Illustrated by Stephanie Boey

PARRAGON

A PARRAGON BOOK

Published by Parragon
13 Whiteladies Road, Clifton, Bristol BS8 1PB

Produced by The Templar Company plc,
Pippbrook Mill, London Road, Dorking, Surrey RH4 1JE

This edition copyright © 1998 Parragon

Designed by Janie Louise Hunt

All rights reserved

Printed in Italy

ISBN 0 75252 605 7

Contents

Meet the Jam Pandas

Jim Jam's Big Day Out

Peaches and Plum in Trouble

GRANDMA

MA AND PA JAM

BIG BAMBOO

JIM JAM

PEACHES AND PLUM

MEET
The Jam Pandas

It was a sunny day when the Jam Pandas arrived at Tumbledown Orchard. There were seven of them altogether — Grandma, Ma and Pa Jam, Big Bamboo their eldest son, Peaches and Plum the young twins, and baby Jim Jam.

The Jam Pandas had been left the cottage and orchard by their Great Uncle Greengage, who was rather an eccentric old panda. He had spent all of his time tending the fruit in the orchard, and had neglected the cottage, which was badly in need of repair. "Never mind," said Grandma cheerfully. "We'll soon smarten it up." "Come along then, everybody," said Pa. "Let's get this truck unloaded."

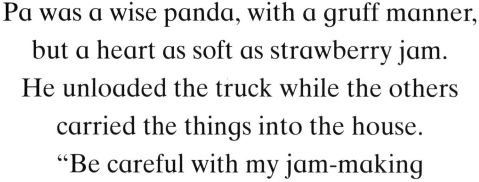

Pa was a wise panda, with a gruff manner,
but a heart as soft as strawberry jam.
He unloaded the truck while the others
carried the things into the house.
"Be careful with my jam-making
equipment!" said Grandma. Grandma was
known far and wide for the delicious jams
she made. "I shall soon be making jam with
all the lovely fruit from the orchard, "
she said happily. "I wonder if there
is a strawberry patch?"
Every Jam Panda had their own
favourite flavour of jam. Grandma's was
strawberry and Pa's was pear.

Soon everything was unloaded, and Ma set about organizing the clean up. Everyone was given a job to do. "This place needs scrubbing from top to bottom!" she said briskly. In no time at all, floors were being scrubbed, carpets were being beaten and feather dusters were flying over the dusty furniture. "I think I'll have earned a nice raspberry jam sandwich after all this hard work," puffed Ma. (*You can guess what flavour jam Ma liked!*)

Ma knew that the cheeky young Jam Panda twins, Peaches and Plum, wanted to explore the rest of the house, so she sent them to look for a good place to store all the jars of jam they had brought with them. The excited little pandas searched through every room in the house, opening cupboards and drawers. The old rooms were dark and dusty and full of cobwebs — just right for hiding in and jumping out on poor Grandma, who was trying to find somewhere to keep her knitting! The terrible twins were always playing tricks and up to mischief.

They chased each other up the stairs.
"Look at me!" cried Peaches, swinging from
the frame of an old four-poster bed.
Soon Peaches and Plum were jumping on
the bed and fighting with the pillows.
Feathers were flying everywhere.
"Jumping Jamspoons!" cried Ma,
coming into the room. "We're supposed
to be cleaning the house, not messing it up!
Go out into the garden and look
after your little brother."

Peaches and Plum went downstairs and into the garden. Their little brother Jim Jam was sitting in the blueberry patch.

There was nothing he liked more than blueberries, especially when they were made into jam! Jim Jam was an adorable little baby panda, who was full of energy. Ma had to keep a close eye on him as he would crawl away whenever he got the chance.

Jim Jam had been eating the berries, and now there was juice running all down his chin. "That looks like fun," said Peaches. Soon the twins were holding a competition to see who could

cram the most blueberries in their mouth at once, and their faces were covered in juice. Just then, Plum looked up. "Uh-oh!" he said, through a mouthful of berries. "Aunt alert!"

Aunt Apricot had arrived with a house-warming gift of an enormous jam sponge. Now she was heading down the garden towards the three young pandas, holding a large handkerchief which she had fished from her handbag. "Jangling jampots! You three are in a jam! Come here and I'll clean you up," she said, licking the corner of her hankie. With that, the three little pandas were off in a flash, heading for the house as fast as their little furry paws could carry them.

Back in the kitchen Big Bamboo, the eldest son, was unpacking all the jam they had brought with them. All of the jars were open, and he looked up guiltily as the rest of the family appeared.

"What are you up to now?" asked Ma, with a sigh.

"Just testing to make sure none of the jam went off during the journey," said Big Bamboo, innocently. He was such a greedy panda, especially when it came to his favourite blackcurrant jam. "Well I think we've all earned some tea," said Ma.

And so the Jam Pandas settled down to the first of many jammy teatimes in their new home at Tumbledown Cottage.

"I think we're going to be happy here," said Grandma.

"So do I," said Big Bamboo. "After all, the blackcurrant patch is enormous!"

JIM JAM'S
Big Day Out

One fine spring morning the Jam Pandas were all having breakfast together at Tumbledown Cottage.

"I will need your help this morning Big Bamboo," said Pa. "We must plant some redcurrant bushes."

"And I have an extremely large batch of strawberry jam to make," said Grandma.

"I'm taking the twins into town to do some shopping," said Ma.

"Jam, jam, jam!" said baby Jim Jam.

"Oh dear," said Ma, looking worried. "Who is going to look after little Jim Jam? We are all too busy!"

"I have an idea," said Pa.
"The marmalade cat can look after him!"
And so it was decided that Jim Jam would
spend the day at the farm where his best
friend the marmalade cat lived.
Jim Jam was very excited.
The marmalade cat often came to
visit him at Tumbledown Cottage,
and had told him lots of things about the
farm and all the animals that lived there,
but Jim Jam had never been to visit.

Pa took Jim Jam to the farm in his big truck, and the marmalade cat met them at the gate. "Take good care of him," said Pa gruffly to the marmalade cat, as he waved goodbye. "And don't get into mischief, Jim Jam!"

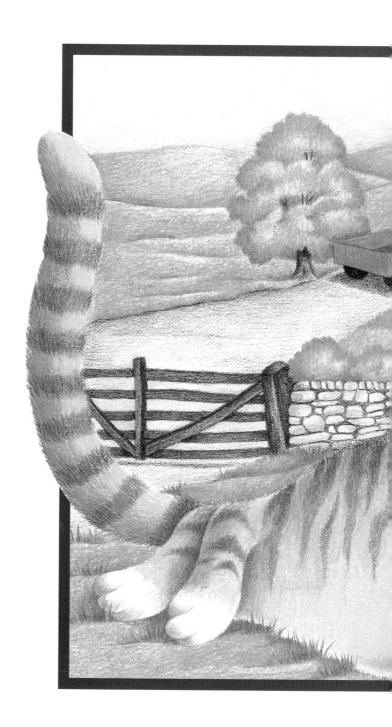

First, the two friends headed into the field full of sheep and little lambs. Jim Jam had never seen lambs before, and he was very excited. He crawled over to take a closer look. Mummy sheep looked up and gave a loud "Baaa!" as Jim Jam approached. She looked rather fierce and Jim Jam felt frightened. He turned and crawled away as fast as he could.

"Don't worry," said the marmalade cat, laughing at Jim Jam's scared face. "She won't hurt you. She is just taking care of her babies."

They carried on towards the duck pond. "Let's go and see the ducks," said the marmalade cat. But as Jim Jam was kneeling down at the edge of the pond, taking a closer look at the fluffy ducklings, mummy duck came up behind him and gave a loud "Quack!" He was so surprised that he fell into the pond with a SPLASH! The marmalade cat soon fished him out, but he was very wet. Poor Jim Jam!

Next, Jim Jam and the marmalade cat went to visit the pigs in the pigpen. Jim Jam wanted to make friends with the piglets, and before the marmalade cat could stop him, he had crawled under the gate, and onto the back of the biggest piglet.

The piglet squealed in alarm, and ran around the pigpen as fast as he could, trying to shake Jim Jam off. "Wheee!" called Jim Jam, before landing BUMP! in a pile of hay.

"Come along," said the marmalade cat. "Let's go and watch the cows being milked in the cowshed. They are much too big for you to ride on. You won't get into trouble there."

But this time it was little Jim Jam who frightened the big cow. She had never seen a panda before. With a loud "moo!" she kicked over the bucket of milk and it splashed all over Jim Jam.

"Oh dear," said the marmalade cat. "You are having a messy day Jim Jam!"

Last of all, they went to the hen house, where all the hens were busy laying eggs. Jim Jam liked the hens and the funny clucking sound they made and he was having a lovely time playing with the fluffy yellow chicks, when all of a sudden one of the hens gave a loud squawk and jumped up, knocking some eggs off the shelf. The eggs fell and broke on Jim Jam's head! A big fox was peering through the open door.

Little Jim Jam looked up and saw the fox. Inquisitive as ever, he decided to take a closer look, so he crawled across the hen house towards him. The fox took one look at Jim

Jam, turned on his tail and ran into the distance. The hens squawked with delight. Jim Jam had saved them!

"You really are quite a sight Jim Jam," laughed the marmalade cat. "No wonder you frightened the fox away!"

Back at the farm house, the marmalade cat soon cleaned Jim Jam up, and then he made sure that Jim Jam had a jammy tea to remember, with his favourite blueberry jam. All of Jim Jam's new friends from the farmyard crowded round him, and it turned into quite a celebration.

Just then Pa Jam arrived to take Jim Jam home.

"Have you been good?" asked Pa, sternly.

"He's been just *purrfect*!" said the marmalade cat, with a wink!

PEACHES AND PLUM
In Trouble

It was a bright sunny morning at
Tumbledown Cottage and Grandma was
making a special batch of jam
just for breakfast.
"Can we have some?" cried Peaches
and Plum.

Just then Pa Jam ambled into the kitchen.

"Still eating breakfast?" he grumbled. "You should be up and about like the rest of us. I've been working in the garden since six o'clock this morning."

"So have we," whispered Peaches to Plum, with a giggle. Little did Pa know, but the naughty twins had been out in the garden early too. They had decided to play a trick on him.

Peaches and Plum were two of the cheekiest little pandas you could imagine. They were always up to mischief. Early that morning they had taken Pa's prize pears from the garden shed and hidden them. They knew that he would think Big Bamboo had eaten them. Pa had been planning to enter the pears in the Fruitgrower's Annual Show and he was very proud of them.

After breakfast, Peaches and Plum crept into the garden, hid behind a big raspberry bush and waited to see what would happen.

Their elder brother, Big Bamboo, was pretending to be hard at work as usual. But whenever Pa went off to fetch something, he would sneak into the blackcurrant patch for a crafty jam sandwich. He always kept a supply of them in his pocket, just in case of emergencies.

He had just finished tucking into a large blackcurrant jam sandwich and was having a quiet snooze, when all of a sudden he woke with a start. Pa was thundering down the garden towards him, shouting his name very loudly indeed! Big Bamboo shot to his feet.

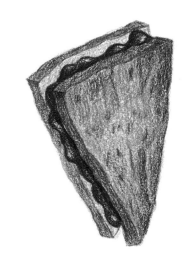

Big Bamboo didn't know why Pa looked so cross, but he wasn't going to stay around to find out! He started to run as fast as he could through the orchard. "You've gone too far this time, you greedy panda," called Pa running behind him. "You'll be sorry when I catch up with you!" Big Bamboo ran faster...

And
faster!

In fact he ran so fast, that when he reached the stream at the end of the orchard he couldn't stop running in time, and he fell in with a great big SPLASH! "Help!" he called. "Get me out!"

Just as Pa was about to say that it served
Big Bamboo right for eating his prize pears,
he heard a loud giggle from behind the
raspberry bush. "Who is that giggling?"
he asked. "Out you come!" Peaches and Plum
came out from behind the bush looking very
guilty and blushing pink. "Do you two terrors
know where my prize pears are?"
asked Pa sternly.

Although Peaches and Plum were naughty, they did not tell lies. "We hid your pears," said Peaches, owning up. "We're very sorry. We didn't think you'd be so cross."

"We didn't damage them," said Plum. "They are in some flowerpots in the potting shed." "Let's go and take a look," said Pa.

Pa and the twins started to head back through the orchard.

"Hey!" called Big Bamboo from the stream. "What about me!" They had forgotten all about helping him!

Soon Big Bamboo had been pulled shivering from the chilly water. Pa apologised for blaming him before finding out the truth about the pears. He sent him to the kitchen to dry off and have an extra large helping of blackcurrant jam to make him feel better.

As for the twins, they were not allowed
any jam for a whole week!
And what of Pa's prize pears? They were
none the worse for their adventure, and won
first prize at the Fruitgrower's Annual Show!

• THE END •